MYSTERIES BEYOND KNOWLEDGE

SRINIVAS KRISHNAN

Copyright © Srinivas Krishnan 2024
All Rights Reserved.

ISBN 979-8-89277-595-3

This book has been published with all efforts taken to make the material error-free after the consent of the author. However, the author and the publisher do not assume and hereby disclaim any liability to any party for any loss, damage, or disruption caused by errors or omissions, whether such errors or omissions result from negligence, accident, or any other cause.

While every effort has been made to avoid any mistake or omission, this publication is being sold on the condition and understanding that neither the author nor the publishers or printers would be liable in any manner to any person by reason of any mistake or omission in this publication or for any action taken or omitted to be taken or advice rendered or accepted on the basis of this work. For any defect in printing or binding the publishers will be liable only to replace the defective copy by another copy of this work then available.

Acknowledgement

"In the boundless tapestry of existence, the keys to enlightenment and the secrets of power are woven into the very fabric of our understanding. As we unravel the transcendent laws, we discover the limitless potential within ourselves, and in that discovery, we find the power to shape the destiny of worlds.

This book is an impassioned tribute to my beloved family, the very reason my existence knows no bounds, forever entwined with their enduring love."

~ Srinivas Krishnan ~

Contents

Contents

Prologue

"Serpentine Scroll"

It was a brisk autumn evening when Sydney Korale, a renowned scientist with an insatiable curiosity, stumbled upon an ancient manuscript hidden deep within the archives of an obscure library. The library, tucked away in the heart of a forgotten town, had long been abandoned by those seeking knowledge, its secrets buried beneath layers of dust and neglect.

Sydney had dedicated his life to the pursuit of understanding the laws that governed the universe. His laboratory was a testament to his relentless quest for knowledge, filled with complex instruments and journals brimming with equations. Yet, despite his numerous accomplishments in the world of science, there was a persistent yearning within him—a yearning to unravel the mysteries that lay beyond the boundaries of empirical research.

On that fateful evening, as Sydney leafed through the pages of the manuscript, he discovered a revelation that would set in motion a journey unlike any he had ever embarked upon. The document, handwritten in elegant script on aged parchment, bore the title,

"The Shadow's Script: Key Tenets of a Transcendent Being."

The manuscript contained 17 enigmatic laws, each a profound insight into the nature of existence itself. These laws hinted at a reality beyond the realm of conventional science, a reality that seemed to bridge the gap between spirituality and the physical world. Sydney's scientific mind buzzed with excitement as he read through the intricate descriptions of these laws:

1. "Energy is the Primeval Life Force of Existence."

2. "The Law of Objects – All objects in this Universe are made out of energy."

3. "The Law of Awareness: Awareness is aware of Experience."

4. "The Thought Theorem: Thought is considered as the inception of any means of communication."

5. "The Law of Communication: 7% is Verbal and 93% is non-verbal."

6. "The Brain-Heart Theory: All communication starts from the mind and ends in the mind."

7. "The Law of Scientific Prayer: Scientific prayer is the harmonious interaction of the conscious & sub-conscious levels of mind."

8. "The Law of Data Availability: Data becomes available to a human for consumption & digestion at the very precise moment it is needed."

9. "The Law of Synchronicity: Everything occurs specifically & is mathematically precise."

10. "The Law of Chaining: You can link unrelated people & events together through data."

11. "The Law of Action: All beings act with the best (optimal) intentions based on the data available to them at present."

12. "The Law of Lovelies: Love (Agape) is Eternal, Unconditional, Universal & Timeless."

13. "The Theorem of Divinity: God is an extension of human beings and vice versa."

14. "The Library of Universal Data: Information of the entire Universe is locked within each and every human being."

15. "The Law of the Multiverse: Fate & Destiny are inter-related."

16. "The Law of Future Events: One's future events can be predicted with great accuracy."

17. "The Law of Perfect Imperfection: The Universe is manifested exactly as it should."

As Sydney delved deeper into the manuscript, he felt a growing sense of wonder and unease. These laws hinted at a reality that challenged his scientific beliefs. They spoke of a world where energy, awareness, and communication were interconnected in ways he had never imagined. The manuscript hinted at a profound truth—that the universe was a tapestry of intricately woven threads, each governed by these mysterious laws.

Little did Sydney know that his pursuit of knowledge would thrust him into a world of intrigue and danger. He would soon come face to face with Victor Kandle, an enigmatic antagonist who sought to harness the power of these laws for his own malevolent purposes. Their clash would become a battle between science and spirituality, reason, and intuition, and ultimately, the fate of the universe itself.

As Sydney closed the ancient manuscript, he made a decision that would alter the course of his life forever. He would embark on a journey to unravel the secrets of these 17 key tenets, a journey that would take him to the very edge of reality and challenge the boundaries of human understanding. The enigmatic laws were now his guiding light, and he was determined to unlock their profound mysteries.

Chapter 1

"Revealing the Essence"

In the dimly lit confines of his cluttered laboratory, Sydney Korale couldn't shake the feeling of excitement and trepidation that had gripped him ever since he discovered the ancient manuscript. The words of the manuscript echoed in his mind, and he was determined to unravel the mysteries it held.

The chapter began with Sydney immersing himself in the first law, "Energy is the Primeval Life Force of Existence." He spent countless hours studying the properties of energy, conducting experiments, and consulting his extensive library of scientific texts. Energy, he realized, was the foundation of everything in the universe, a force that existed in various forms and vibrated at different frequencies.

As Sydney delved deeper into his research, he encountered fascinating phenomena that seemed to align with the first law. He observed the transfer of energy in chemical reactions, the conversion of electrical energy into mechanical motion, and the radiant energy of the sun that sustained life on Earth.

It was as if the entire cosmos pulsed with the rhythm of energy.

But it wasn't just the physical aspects of energy that intrigued him. Sydney began to explore the implications of the first law on consciousness and awareness. He pondered the idea that human consciousness itself might be a manifestation of this primordial energy, and that awareness was a function of energy.

As Sydney continued his investigations, he encountered strange occurrences that hinted at the interconnectedness of all things. In his laboratory, he observed how energy from one object seemed to influence the behaviour of another, even when they were physically separated. It was as if the manuscript's assertion that all objects were connected through intertwining energy was coming to life before his eyes.

Sydney stood at the precipice of a profound revelation. He had glimpsed the intricate tapestry of energy that wove through the fabric of the universe, but he knew that this was only the beginning of his journey. The ancient manuscript had hinted at seventeen key tenets, and he was determined to unlock the secrets of each one.

Little did Sydney know that his pursuit of knowledge would lead him to even more enigmatic discoveries, challenge his beliefs, and eventually, bring him face to face with the malevolent Victor Kandle, who was equally determined to harness the power of these laws for his own dark purposes.

With the first law of the transcendent beings unveiled, Sydney Korale's journey had only just begun, and the mysteries of the universe beckoned him deeper into the unknown.

Chapter 2

"Intertwining of Inanimate and Animate"

After Sydney Korale's deep dive into the mysteries of energy, he was eager to explore the second law of the transcendent beings: "The Law of Objects – All objects in this Universe are made out of energy vibrating at various frequencies."

Sydney's laboratory buzzed with anticipation as he meticulously prepared for his next series of experiments. He had become obsessed with the notion that even inanimate objects possessed a hidden sentience, as hinted at by the manuscript. Armed with his scientific instruments and a determination to uncover the truth, he began a series of tests.

In the early days of his research, Sydney focused on animate objects – living organisms such as plants, animals, and humans. He observed how energy flowed through these organisms, sustaining life, and allowing them to interact with their environment. He marvelled at the intricate web of energy that connected all living things, reinforcing the manuscript's assertion of interconnectedness.

But it was when Sydney turned his attention to inanimate objects that the plot took an unexpected twist. He set up experiments with seemingly mundane objects – a chair, a book, and a glass of water. To his astonishment, he noticed subtle changes in their behaviour when he introduced variations in energy levels.

The chair, for instance, seemed to shift its position ever so slightly when exposed to different frequencies of energy. The book's pages turned as if reacting to an unseen force, and the water in the glass exhibited peculiar ripples when subjected to specific energy patterns.

Sydney was on the verge of a ground-breaking discovery – the idea that even inanimate objects possessed a form of energy-based consciousness. It was a concept that challenged the very foundations of science and philosophy. If objects could respond to energy, could they, in some way, be aware of their surroundings?

As Sydney contemplated the implications of his findings, a chilling realization dawned upon him. If objects indeed had a form of consciousness, what did this mean for the nature of reality itself? Could the universe be far more sentient and interconnected than he had ever imagined?

Just as Sydney's mind swirled with these mind-bending questions, an unexpected visitor arrived at his laboratory – an enigmatic figure cloaked in shadow. The visitor's voice was a low, menacing whisper as he spoke, "You're treading on dangerous ground, Mr. Korale. The secrets you seek may be more perilous than you can fathom."

Sydney stood face to face with the mysterious visitor, whose presence hinted at a web of intrigue and danger that extended far beyond the confines of his laboratory. As the plot thickened, Sydney realized that his pursuit of knowledge had brought him closer to a malevolent force that sought to control the very essence of existence – the energy that bound all things together.

With the revelation that even inanimate objects might possess a form of consciousness, Sydney Korale's world had shifted, and the boundaries between animate and inanimate, science and mysticism, had blurred. As he embarked on the next phase of his journey, he knew that the answers he sought would lead him to a truth more profound and perilous than he had ever imagined.

Chapter 3

"New Realms of Awareness"

As Sydney Korale delved deeper into the enigmatic manuscript's revelations, he found himself captivated by the third law: "The Law of Awareness: Awareness is aware of Experience." The notion that awareness itself was a fundamental aspect of existence piqued his curiosity like never before.

In the dimly lit laboratory, Sydney's experiments took on a new dimension. He began to explore the nature of awareness within the context of energy, attempting to grasp how consciousness could be both the observer and the observed. His studies led him to contemplate the nature of self-awareness and the profound implications it held for human existence.

As Sydney immersed himself in his research, a new character entered his world – a young scholar named Brian Lawson, known among his peers as Pontifus Maximus. Brian was a recluse, known for his deep knowledge of esoteric and metaphysical subjects. It was rumoured that he held the key to understanding the true nature of awareness.

Their meeting was a stroke of serendipity. Brian had come across Sydney's work in an obscure academic journal and recognized the young scientist's potential. He sought out Sydney, convinced that their paths were destined to intersect. Brian's enigmatic aura and wisdom left Sydney both intrigued and apprehensive.

In Brian's presence, Sydney was introduced to a world beyond the confines of empirical science. Brian spoke of awareness as an eternal, unchanging presence – a state of being that transcended the mind's fleeting thoughts and emotions. He guided Sydney through meditation exercises and philosophical discussions, opening his mind to the possibility that awareness was the unchanging core of existence itself.

As their interactions deepened, Brian hinted at a secret knowledge – a hidden truth that had eluded humanity for centuries. He spoke cryptically of a path toward enlightenment and hinted that Sydney's journey into the manuscript's laws was just the beginning of a profound awakening.

But it was the night when Sydney, in a state of deep meditation, experienced a profound shift in his own awareness that the chapter took an unexpected turn. As he delved into the depths of his own consciousness, he felt a connection – a whisper of something greater, something ancient and profound.

Just as Sydney was about to uncover the hidden meaning behind Brian's cryptic words, the laboratory's door burst open. Victor Kandle, the malevolent antagonist from Sydney's past, stood in the doorway, his eyes gleaming with malice.

With a sinister smile, Victor sneered, "I see you've been exploring the mysteries of awareness, Mr. Korale. How delightful. But be warned, there are depths of consciousness that even the bravest dare not tread."

Victor Kandle's ominous warning hung in the air, leaving Sydney and Brian Lawson at a crossroads. As Victor's presence loomed over them, the plot took an unsettling turn, and Sydney was faced with a choice that would shape the course of his journey. What was the true nature of awareness, and how could it be harnessed? And what hidden agenda did Victor Kandle hold in his relentless pursuit of power?

The next chapter held the promise of answers, but it also carried the weight of impending danger. Sydney Korale's quest for knowledge had led him into uncharted territory, where the boundaries between consciousness and the unknown blurred, and where the presence of a malevolent force threatened to consume all in its path.

Chapter 4

"Illuminating the Thought Theorem"

In the aftermath of Victor Kandle's ominous intrusion, Sydney Korale found himself torn between his relentless pursuit of knowledge and the lurking danger that seemed to follow his every step. Yet, he couldn't quell the burning curiosity that had driven him this far. With determination and a hint of trepidation, he turned his attention to the fourth law in the manuscript: "The Thought Theorem."

As Sydney delved into the mysteries of thought, he realized that this law was no less enigmatic than the previous ones. It stated, "Thought is considered as the inception of any means of communication. All cause & effect are initiated from thought." It seemed to suggest that thought was the very fabric from which the universe wove its intricate tapestry.

To explore this further, Sydney designed a series of experiments that probed the nature of thought itself. He began with the basic premise that thought was the precursor to all actions and interactions. Every invention, every communication, every decision – it all began as a thought in someone's mind.

As Sydney's experiments unfolded, he uncovered a world of intricate connections between thought, energy, and action. He observed how thoughts could be measured as patterns of energy, and how these patterns influenced the behaviour of both animate and inanimate objects. It was as if thoughts were a silent force, shaping the world around us.

But as Sydney delved deeper into the Thought Theorem, he couldn't shake the feeling that someone – or something – or was observing his every move. It was the same lurking presence he had felt back in his laboratory during Victor Kandle's intrusion. The shadowy figure seemed to be one step ahead, always on the periphery of his awareness.

It was during a late-night session in his laboratory that Sydney finally came face to face with the shadowy enigma that had haunted him. The figure stepped out from the darkness, revealing himself as a mysterious operative known as "The Shadow." With an air of cold detachment, The Shadow disclosed his connection to Victor Kandle.

"The Thought Theorem," he explained, "is not just a philosophical concept. It holds the key to unimaginable power, and Victor Kandle seeks to harness it for his own dark purposes. He believes that by controlling thought, he can reshape reality itself."

The revelation left Sydney stunned. The Shadow's warning carried a weight of urgency – Victor Kandle's plans were far more sinister and ambitious than he had initially realized. The battle for the secrets of the transcendent laws had taken a dangerous turn, and Sydney was now entangled in a web of intrigue and peril.

The Shadow had extended a cryptic offer of assistance, hinting at a network of allies who shared Sydney's goal of safeguarding the profound knowledge contained within the manuscript. It was a glimmer of hope in the face of impending danger, but Sydney had to make a choice – to trust in The Shadow's alliance and continue his quest or retreat from the mysteries that threatened to consume him.

With The Shadow's revelation and the impending decisions that lay ahead, Sydney Korale was yet again left at a crossroads, torn between the pursuit of knowledge and the relentless pursuit of power by Victor Kandle. The thought theorem was just the tip of the iceberg, and the true depths of its implications were yet to be unveiled.

Chapter 5

"Vortex of Communication"

With The Shadow's cryptic offer of assistance and Victor Kandle's relentless pursuit of power, Sydney Korale found himself in a precarious situation. He was at a crossroads, torn between two opposing forces – one seeking to harness the transcendent laws for good and the other for dark purposes. The next law in the manuscript, "The Law of Communication," held the promise of unlocking new knowledge that could tip the balance.

Intrigued by the potential of the fifth law, Sydney delved into its mysteries. "All cause & effect are initiated from thought," the manuscript had stated. Sydney realized that communication was the medium through which thoughts and intentions were shared with the world. It was a bridge between the inner realm of thought and the outer world of action.

As Sydney conducted experiments to understand the law of communication, he explored various forms of human interaction, from verbal and written communication to non-verbal cues and body language. He realized that communication was not limited to language but extended to the subtle nuances of expression, tone, and intent.

But the plot took an unexpected twist when Sydney received an encrypted message – a message that seemed to come from The Shadow. The message was a complex code, a puzzle that challenged Sydney's newfound knowledge of the transcendent laws. It was as if The Shadow had presented him with a test, a test that held the key to their alliance.

As Sydney diligently worked to decipher the code, he realized that it contained references to the first four laws he had explored—the laws of energy, objects, awareness, and thought. It was a riddle that demanded he apply his understanding of these laws to unlock its secrets.

The message hinted at a hidden truth – a truth that could alter the course of their mission. It suggested that the laws were not isolated principles but interconnected facets of a greater whole. As Sydney unravelled the code, he discovered a profound revelation – the manuscript contained a hidden narrative, a story within the laws themselves.

With each layer of the code he decrypted, Sydney uncovered fragments of a forgotten history – a history that tied together the transcendent beings, the laws, and the quest for ultimate knowledge. It was a revelation that shook him to his core and left him with more questions than answers.

But just as Sydney thought he had unravelled the entire message; he received a chilling communication. It was Victor Kandle's voice, cold and taunting. "You may think you're close to understanding the laws, Mr. Korale, but there are depths you have yet to fathom. I will stop at nothing to possess their full power."

The plot thickened as Sydney realized that not only was he racing against time to decipher the remaining codes, but he was also locked in a deadly battle of wits with Victor Kandle. The fifth law of communication had revealed a hidden narrative, and Sydney knew that the remaining laws held the key to their ultimate significance.

Sydney was left with a sense of urgency and a burning determination to unravel the mysteries of the manuscript before it fell into the wrong hands. The Shadow's true intentions remained a mystery, and the fate of the transcendent laws hung in the balance.

Chapter 6

"Arcane Insights into the Brain – Heart Theory"

Sydney Korale's relentless pursuit of knowledge had led him into a world of intrigue and peril, where the transcendent laws held the key to both enlightenment and destruction. As he delved into the sixth law, "The Brain – Heart Theory," he couldn't shake the feeling that each revelation brought him closer to understanding the grand tapestry of existence.

The law posited that all communication and understanding began with the conscious mind, but it was the subconscious that played a pivotal role in deciphering and transmitting the messages. Sydney pondered the profound implications of this theory as he continued his experiments and studies.

It was during this chapter that Brian Lawson re-entered Sydney's life, bringing with him a sense of calm and wisdom. Brian had been elusive since their last encounter, but he returned at a critical juncture, sensing that Sydney was on the verge of a breakthrough.

Brian introduced Sydney to his brother, Braandon Lawson, a towering figure known as "The Hammer" due to his imposing physique. Braandon's presence was as imposing as his nickname, but beneath his exterior lay a gentle soul with a deep understanding of the Brain-Heart Theory.

Braandon explained that the Brain-Heart Theory was not limited to individual consciousness but extended to the collective consciousness of humanity. He shared insights from ancient traditions and modern neuroscience, showing how the conscious mind acted as the gatekeeper of thoughts, while the subconscious served as the channel for deeper understanding.

As Sydney listened to Braandon's teachings, he began to grasp the concept that the conscious mind was the surface, constantly interpreting and analysing the world, while the subconscious was the silent observer, absorbing information and sending it to the heart for processing.

But the plot took an unexpected twist when Braandon revealed that the manuscript contained a hidden code – a code that connected the laws in ways Sydney had not yet realized. Each law was like a piece of a puzzle, and the Brain-Heart Theory was the key to deciphering their interdependence.

With Braandon's guidance, Sydney embarked on a journey of introspection and meditation, seeking to connect with his own subconscious and unlock the hidden code within himself. It was a journey that would test his resolve and push the boundaries of his understanding.

As Sydney delved deeper into his own consciousness, he began to sense a resonance – a connection to something greater, something that transcended the individual and tapped into the collective consciousness of humanity. It was a revelation that left him humbled and awestruck.

But just as Sydney felt he was on the verge of a breakthrough, a message arrived – a message from The Shadow. The enigmatic operative warned Sydney that Victor Kandle was closing in, driven by an insatiable hunger for power.

With the sixth law of the Brain-Heart Theory revealing new layers of understanding, Sydney faced a dilemma. He had glimpsed the hidden code within himself, but he knew that the true power of the transcendent laws lay in their interconnectedness. The fate of the manuscript and the balance of power hung in the balance, and Sydney had to make a choice – continue his quest for enlightenment or confront the looming threat of Victor Kandle.

The enigma of the transcendent laws deepened, and Sydney's journey led him further into the heart of the mysteries that held the universe together. With Brian,

Braandon, and The Shadow as his allies, he stood on the precipice of a revelation that could change the course of history.

Chapter 7

"Strategies for Scientific Prayer"

While Sydney Korale continued his quest to unravel the transcendent laws, Victor Kandle, the malevolent antagonist, was not idle. He was determined to harness the power of the laws for his dark ambitions, and to achieve that, he enlisted the aid of two enigmatic entities – Anika Bingham and Davillia Bonham.

Anika Bingham was Victor's angelic accomplice, a being of celestial beauty and cunning intellect. She had once served as a guardian spirit, but her fall from grace had twisted her into a formidable ally for Victor. With her ethereal charm and manipulative nature, Anika was the perfect instrument to sow chaos within Sydney's exploration.

Davillia Bonham, on the other hand, was Victor's demon, a creature of malevolence and deceit. She had existed in the shadowy realms of the infernal, and her alliance with Victor granted her a chance to wreak havoc in the human world. Davillia's dark influence could penetrate the minds of the vulnerable and fuel their fears and desires.

As Sydney delved into the seventh law, "The Law of Scientific Prayer," he explored the concept of harnessing the infinite power within humans through prayer. This law posited that scientific prayer was the harmonious interaction of the conscious and subconscious levels of the mind, scientifically directed toward a specific purpose.

Sydney conducted experiments to test the power of focused intent and prayer, seeking to understand how it could unlock access to the infinite potential within each individual. He believed that prayer, when approached with scientific precision, could be a force for positive change in the world.

But Victor, Anika, and Davillia had other plans. They conspired to manipulate Sydney's experiments, subtly altering the data and the results to create confusion and doubt. Anika whispered deceptive thoughts into the minds of those assisting Sydney, while Davillia stoked their insecurities and fears.

The chapter unfolded as a battle of wills between Sydney and the malevolent trio. Sydney's determination to unlock the true potential of scientific prayer clashed with Victor's relentless pursuit of power. Anika and Davillia's covert interference added layers of complexity to the struggle.

Amid the chaos, Sydney began to sense that his experiments were yielding inconsistent results.

The very nature of scientific prayer was elusive, and the interference of Anika and Davillia blurred the line between intention and manipulation.

But Sydney's tenacity and growing awareness allowed him to see through the deception. He recognized the subtle signs of interference and began to formulate countermeasures. With each revelation, he inched closer to understanding the true power of scientific prayer.

As the chapter reached its climax, Sydney confronted Victor Kandle, accusing him of manipulating the experiments. Victor, however, remained unfazed, revelling in the chaos he had sown. He taunted Sydney, challenging him to continue his pursuit, knowing that the next law held the key to even greater power.

With the seventh law of scientific prayer in action, the battle between good and malevolence escalated. Sydney Korale stood at a crossroads, armed with newfound awareness, and Victor Kandle continued to plot in the shadows, driven by a thirst for power that knew no bounds. The transcendent laws held the fate of humanity in their balance, and the battle for their understanding raged on.

Chapter 8

"Kaleidoscope of Data Availability"

As Sydney Korale's quest to unlock the mysteries of the transcendent laws intensified, he found himself in a pivotal moment in his journey. The enigmatic operative known as The Shadow had once again emerged from the shadows, casting an intriguing light on his own elusive nature.

The Shadow revealed a bit more of his enigmatic identity, offering Sydney glimpses into his past and the motivations that had led him to protect the transcendent laws. However, his true origins and ultimate purpose remained shrouded in mystery.

The Shadow presented Sydney with a unique and catchy object – a small, intricately crafted hourglass. It was unlike any ordinary timepiece, and The Shadow referred to it as the "Sands of Destiny." This enigmatic device held the key to unlocking the secrets of the eighth law, "The Law of Data Availability."

The eighth law posited that data became available to a human for consumption and digestion at the precise moment it was needed. Sydney had already encountered the concept of synchronicity, where the universe guided individuals toward the data they required. Now, with the Sands of Destiny in his possession, he was about to delve deeper into this concept.

The Shadow explained that the Sands of Destiny had the ability to manipulate time and space, allowing the possessor to access the data they needed at the exact moment of relevance. It was a tool of unparalleled power, but it came with great responsibility.

To harness the Sands of Destiny effectively and unlock the eighth law, Sydney needed to attune himself to its unique frequencies. The Shadow guided him through a series of meditations and exercises, teaching him to synchronize his consciousness with the device.

As Sydney's connection to the Sands of Destiny deepened, he began to perceive the subtle shifts in time and space. He could foresee events before they occurred, accessing information and knowledge as if it had always been at his fingertips. It was a profound and exhilarating experience that expanded his understanding of data availability.

Yet, as Sydney delved deeper into the eighth law, he couldn't help but wonder about the implications of such power. The Sands of Destiny allowed him to access data from the past, present, and future, blurring the lines of reality and perception.

The chapter unfolded with Sydney's growing proficiency in utilizing the Sands of Destiny, guided by The Shadow's enigmatic wisdom. Together, they explored the intricacies of data availability and the role it played in shaping the course of events.

But even as Sydney gained new insights, The Shadow's mysterious aura remained intact. He continued to guard his true identity and ultimate purpose, leaving Sydney with unanswered questions.

As the chapter concluded, Sydney stood on the threshold of a revelation – one that would not only unlock the secrets of the eighth law but also bring him closer to understanding the transcendent laws as a whole. The Sands of Destiny was both a gift and a responsibility, and Sydney had yet to fathom the depths of its potential.

Chapter 9

"Rhythms of Synchronicity"

As Sydney Korale's understanding of the transcendent laws deepened, he found himself embroiled in a complex web of allies and adversaries. The enigmatic figures, Anika Bingham and Davillia Bonham, continued to play their part in Victor Kandle's scheme to disrupt Sydney's exploration.

Anika Bingham, with her celestial beauty and manipulative charm, had taken a keen interest in Brian and Braandon Lawson. She insinuated herself into their lives, sowing seeds of doubt and discord. Brian, ever the seeker of wisdom, was drawn to her ethereal presence, while Braandon, known as "The Hammer," remained suspicious of her intentions.

Davillia Bonham, the malevolent demon in Victor Kandle's service, had chosen to target Braandon, recognizing his towering physique and protective nature as a potential weakness. She whispered dark desires and fears into his mind, exploiting his inner conflicts.

As Sydney contemplated the ninth law, "The Law of Synchronicity," he delved into the concept that everything occurred with mathematical precision, and there was no such thing as coincidence. Synchronicity, he realized, was the guiding force that orchestrated events with purpose and intent.

It was during this contemplation that Sydney was introduced to a holographic character named Grovit Lipton. Grovit appeared as a spectral figure, a digital entity that materialized before Sydney. Grovit explained that he was a manifestation of the ninth law, a sentient representation of the law of synchronicity itself.

Grovit Lipton guided Sydney through a series of experiences that demonstrated the profound interconnectedness of all things. He showed Sydney how seemingly unrelated events and occurrences were intricately linked by the invisible threads of synchronicity. Sydney witnessed the unfolding of events that led to significant discoveries, chance encounters, and life-changing moments.

But as Sydney delved deeper into the mysteries of synchronicity, he couldn't escape the malevolent influence of Amethyst and Davillia. The dark duo continued to manipulate the lives of those around him, causing rifts and turmoil among his allies. Sydney realized that their actions were intricately woven into the tapestry of synchronicity, testing his resolve, and pushing him to the limits of his understanding.

The chapter unfolded as a delicate balance between the revelations of synchronicity and the insidious machinations of Amethyst and Davillia. Sydney's journey into the ninth law brought him closer to comprehending the hidden patterns of the universe, but it also revealed the complexity of the forces at play.

Sydney faced the daunting task of unravelling the intricacies of synchronicity while navigating the treacherous web of manipulation and deceit woven by his malevolent adversaries. The transcendent laws held both enlightenment and peril, and Sydney's quest was far from over.

Chapter 10

"Infinity within Chaining"

As Sydney Korale delved deeper into his exploration of the transcendent laws, he found himself face to face with the tenth tenet, "The Law of Chaining." This law posited that one could link seemingly unrelated people and events together through data, creating a chain of interconnected experiences and knowledge.

Sydney's journey had already revealed the intricate dance of synchronicity and data availability, but the tenth law took it a step further. It suggested that individuals could actively manipulate the chain of events through conscious intent, using data as the medium to connect disparate elements.

Amidst his contemplation of this law, The Shadow emerged once more from the shadows, his enigmatic presence casting a surreal atmosphere over the unfolding events. He seemed to appear at moments of crucial revelation, guiding Sydney on his quest.

The Shadow revealed another piece of important information – details about the true nature of Victor Kandle's ambitions. He explained that Victor sought to manipulate the transcendent laws not for enlightenment or the betterment of humanity but for personal gain and power beyond imagination.

The Shadow's revelations painted a bleak picture of Victor's intentions, highlighting the danger he posed to the delicate balance of the universe. It was clear that Victor's thirst for power knew no bounds, and he was willing to go to any lengths to achieve his goals.

Sydney realized that he was not merely on a quest for knowledge but a mission to prevent Victor from unleashing chaos upon the world. The tenth law, "The Law of Chaining," took on a new significance as he understood that his ability to connect people, events, and data could be a powerful tool in thwarting Victor's sinister plans.

With The Shadow's guidance, Sydney began to master the art of chaining, learning how to forge connections and manipulate data to create a network of information. He recognized that by strategically linking key elements, he could disrupt Victor's machinations and protect the transcendent laws from falling into the wrong hands.

The chapter unfolded with Sydney's growing proficiency in the tenth law, intertwining his efforts to thwart Victor with The Shadow's cryptic revelations. As he delved deeper into the intricacies of chaining, he realized that each link in the chain had the potential to unravel Victor's carefully laid schemes.

Yet, The Shadow remained elusive, guarding his true identity and the full extent of his knowledge. He continued to provide guidance, but his enigmatic nature left Sydney with more questions than answers.

Sydney stood on the precipice of a decision – to embrace the power of chaining and confront Victor Kandle head-on or to continue his quest for enlightenment, knowing that the fate of the transcendent laws hung in the balance. The tenth law had unveiled new possibilities, but it also presented a formidable challenge, and Sydney was determined to face it head-on.

Chapter 11

"Spark of Action"

In his continuing quest to understand the transcendent laws, Sydney Korale found himself at the threshold of the eleventh law, "The Law of Action." This law posited that all beings acted with the best intentions based on the data available to them at the present moment.

As Sydney contemplated the intricacies of this law, he encountered a new character named Timothy Turnbull, affectionately known as "Haystacks" due to his vivid imagination and remarkable ability to articulate events with a high degree of accuracy. Haystacks had a unique gift for deciphering the intricacies of human behaviours and the actions driven by data and intent.

Haystacks' relationship with Sydney was deep and profound. They had crossed paths during their respective journeys to unravel the transcendent laws, and their connection was born out of a shared desire for understanding and enlightenment. Haystacks' ability to analyse and interpret actions complemented Sydney's quest to master the laws.

In this chapter, the relationship between Haystacks and Grovit Lipton, the holographic character representing the eighth law, became evident. Haystacks possessed a rare talent—he could translate Grovit's holographic projections into coherent narratives and actionable insights. Grovit's abstract teachings found clarity and purpose through Haystacks' interpretations.

Together, Haystacks and Grovit became invaluable guides for Sydney as he navigated the complexities of the eleventh law. They helped him recognize that actions, while driven by data and intent, were not always executed flawlessly. Intentions could be pure, but execution might be flawed, leading to unintended consequences.

Sydney's journey through the eleventh law unveiled the concept that controlling data could influence the actions of individuals. By understanding the motivations and data that drove people's actions, one could influence outcomes and guide events in a desired direction.

Yet, the malevolent Victor Kandle remained a looming threat, determined to exploit the laws for his own gain. Anika Bingham and Davillia Bonham continued to play their roles, weaving a web of manipulation and discord. But Haystacks and Grovit proved to be formidable allies in Sydney's struggle against Victor's machinations.

The chapter unfolded as Sydney, Haystacks, and Grovit collaborated to decipher the intricacies of the eleventh law. They explored the delicate balance between intention and execution, recognizing that the best of intentions could sometimes lead to unforeseen consequences.

As the chapter concluded, Sydney stood on the precipice of a revelation – that actions, driven by data and intent, were the tangible manifestations of the transcendent laws. With Haystacks and Grovit by his side, he was better equipped to navigate the intricate dance of actions and their consequences.

Despite the malevolent pursuit of Victor Kandle, Sydney Korale was determined to harness the knowledge of the transcendent laws for the greater good. The eleventh law had unveiled the power of understanding and influencing actions, and Sydney was ready to embrace this newfound insight in his ongoing quest for enlightenment.

Chapter 12

"Hummingbird Lovelies"

As Sydney Korale's journey through the transcendent laws continued, he found himself facing a grave crisis. Brian and Braandon Lawson, his trusted companions, were in imminent danger. Victor Kandle's malevolent pursuits had escalated, putting their lives at risk.

The twelfth law, "The Law of Lovelies," had been a source of solace and strength for Sydney throughout his exploration. This law posited that love, in its purest form – Agape – was eternal, unconditional, universal, and timeless. It transcended all beings and was focused on the greater consciousness.

Sydney understood that love was not just an emotion but a powerful force that connected all living things. It was the essence of empathy, compassion, and unity – a force that could drive individuals to great lengths to protect those they cherished.

As the chapter unfolded, Sydney attempted to use the twelfth law to save Brian and Braandon from the clutches of danger. He poured his love and intentions into the universe, seeking a way to ensure their safety. However, despite his unwavering love and pure intentions, he was met with a sense of powerlessness as he struggled to find a solution.

Desperate to save his friends, Sydney turned to his trusted minions, Ava Kristal, and Tara Krishana, for assistance. Together, they brainstormed and sought a solution that could harness the power of the twelfth law to rescue Brian and Braandon from their perilous situation.

Ava and Tara, with their unique abilities and deep understanding of the transcendent laws, proposed a plan rooted in the concept of data availability and love's timeless nature. They suggested that Sydney could use the knowledge he had gained to create a powerful message – a message infused with his love for Brian and Braandon.

This message would transcend time and space, reaching them in their moment of need. It would serve as a beacon of hope and protection, guided by the twelfth law's belief in the timeless and universal nature of love.

Sydney, Ava, and Tara worked tirelessly to craft this message, infusing it with their love and intentions. They released it into the universe, trusting that the twelfth law would ensure its delivery to Brian and Braandon, no matter where they were.

Sydney's hope and determination were rekindled. The power of the twelfth law had provided a glimmer of hope, and he was prepared to face whatever challenges lay ahead to ensure the safety of his beloved friends. With Ava and Tara by his side, he was ready to confront Victor Kandle's malevolent pursuits and protect those he cherished most.

Chapter 13

"Nexus of Divinity"

As Sydney Korale, Ava Kristal, and Tara Krishana worked tirelessly to harness the power of the twelfth law to save Brian and Braandon Lawson, they found themselves in a race against time. The malevolent Victor Kandle had placed their friends in imminent danger, and the clock was ticking.

The thirteenth law, "The Theorem of Divinity," had been on Sydney's mind throughout his journey. It posited that divinity was not an external entity but an extension of human beings and vice versa. God, in this context, was not a separate entity but a collective consciousness, greater than any individual.

In their quest to rescue Brian and Braandon, Sydney, Ava, and Tara sought to tap into this collective consciousness, believing that the power of divinity could provide the guidance and strength they needed. They knew that divinity resided within them, waiting to be awakened.

As the chapter unfolded, they discovered that Grovit Lipton and Timothy "Haystacks" Turnbull held the key to unlocking the thirteenth law. Grovit's holographic projections and Haystacks' remarkable ability to articulate events with precision combined to create a bridge between the human experience and the realm of divinity.

With their guidance, Sydney, Ava, and Tara delved into a state of deep meditation, connecting with the collective consciousness within and without. They sought to access the wisdom of divinity to rescue their friends and thwart Victor Kandle's malevolent plans.

In this heightened state of consciousness, they discovered a profound truth – the divinity they sought was not external but an inherent part of their being. It was a source of strength and clarity, empowering them to act with unwavering purpose.

With newfound determination, Sydney, Ava, and Tara forged a plan rooted in the thirteenth law. They unleashed a torrent of intention and love, infused with the divinity that resided within them. This powerful force created a ripple effect, connecting with the hearts and minds of all who shared in the collective consciousness.

The impact was immediate. Brian and Braandon, who had been ensnared by Victor Kandle's malevolent machinations, felt a surge of hope and protection wash over them. It was as if a divine presence had intervened, guiding them to safety and freedom.

In this chapter, the power of divinity became palpable, as Sydney, Ava, and Tara harnessed its strength to rescue their friends. Grovit and Haystacks, with their unique abilities, played a pivotal role in bridging the gap between the human experience and the realm of divinity.

Brian and Braandon were saved from danger, their lives preserved by the unwavering love, intention, and divinity that bound their friends together. Sydney Korale's journey through the transcendent laws had reached a critical juncture, as he recognized that divinity was not an external force but a wellspring of strength and guidance within. With this revelation, he was prepared to face the challenges that lay ahead in his quest for enlightenment and the protection of the transcendent laws.

Chapter 14

"Almanac of Universal Data"

As Sydney Korale's journey through the transcendent laws continued, he found himself facing a moment of reckoning. The malevolent Victor Kandle and the mysterious Shadow collided in a cataclysmic clash that shook the very foundations of their reality. Sydney stood on the sidelines, helpless in the face of this powerful confrontation.

The fourteenth law, "The Library of Universal Data," had been a source of intrigue and mystery throughout Sydney's exploration. It posited that information of the entire universe, past, present, and future, was locked within each and every human being. Extracting this information without experiencing it firsthand was almost impossible, yet, plausible.

In the midst of the chaotic clash between Victor Kandle and The Shadow, Sydney realized that he needed to tap into the depths of the fourteenth law to understand the true nature of their conflict. He recognized that the answers he sought lay within the vast repository of universal data hidden within himself.

As the chapter unfolded, the confrontation between Victor and The Shadow raged on, each representing opposing forces that threatened the balance of the universe. Sydney watched in awe and fear as the two enigmatic figures clashed with a ferocity that defied comprehension.

Sydney's sense of helplessness grew as he grappled with the magnitude of the situation. He knew that to intervene directly would be futile; he lacked the power to control the outcome of this cosmic struggle. In his moment of despair, he confided in the fourteenth law, seeking guidance from the universal data that resided within him.

With his mind open to the infinite possibilities of the universe, Sydney delved deep into his own consciousness. He began to tap into the vast repository of information and experiences that were part of his own unique journey. The library of universal data became his source of inspiration and insight.

Yet, as he ventured further into this enigmatic realm, he encountered a plot twist that sent shockwaves through his understanding of the transcendent laws. The data he accessed revealed a hidden truth – that The Shadow and Victor Kandle were not mere adversaries but two aspects of a greater cosmic balance.

Their conflict was not about good versus evil but a dance of opposing forces necessary for the equilibrium of the universe. It was a revelation that challenged Sydney's perceptions and forced him to reconsider the nature of his quest.

As the chapter concluded, Sydney grappled with this newfound understanding, torn between his desire to protect the transcendent laws and the realization that the laws themselves were part of a greater cosmic design. The cliff-hanger at the end of the chapter left Sydney with a profound sense of uncertainty, as the true nature of the universe's balance hung in the balance, waiting to be unveiled.

Chapter 15

"Navigating Multiversal Realms"

As Sydney Korale grappled with the revelation that The Shadow and Victor Kandle represented opposing forces necessary for the equilibrium of the universe, a new character emerged – Thunder Penguin, also known as TP. TP, was a long-lost twin of Tara Krishana, and his arrival brought with it a fresh perspective on the transcendent laws.

TP's unique background and connection to Tara made him a valuable addition to the group. He had spent his life exploring the mysteries of the multiverse and had come to believe that the fifteenth law, "The Law of the Multiverse," held the key to uncovering the truth behind the enigmatic Shadow and Victor Kandle.

The fifteenth law posited that fate and destiny were interrelated, with everything predetermined based on the path taken. Yet, there was an infinite number of paths to choose from at any given moment, and each choice led to a new fate. The permutations of the multiverse made the future unpredictable.

With TP's arrival, Sydney was eager to explore this law further in the hopes of understanding the true nature of The Shadow. Together with Haystacks, who had a knack for articulating complex ideas with precision, they delved into The Shadow's background, seeking answers that would forever change the course of their quest.

As the chapter unfolded, TP and Haystacks began to uncover unsettling truths about The Shadow's origins. It became apparent that The Shadow was not who he seemed to be. He was not a force of malevolence but a guardian of the multiverse, tasked with maintaining the delicate balance between opposing forces.

The Shadow's true purpose was to ensure that the multiverse remained stable, even if it meant assuming an enigmatic and intimidating persona. His actions, though seemingly sinister, were driven by a deep sense of duty and a commitment to the greater cosmic design.

Sydney, TP, and Haystacks were left in awe of this revelation. The multiverse's intricate dance of fate and destiny had given rise to The Shadow's existence, and his role was one of profound significance. Their understanding of the transcendent laws was forever altered, as they came to realize that the quest for truth was not always as straightforward as it seemed.

The chapter concluded with Sydney, TP, and Haystacks standing on the precipice of a new reality – one where The Shadow's true nature was unveiled, and their pursuit of enlightenment took on a deeper and more complex dimension. The unsettling plot twist had challenged their perceptions and left them questioning the very nature of their quest and their destinies.

Chapter 16

"Glimpses into Future Events"

As Sydney Korale's quest for truth and enlightenment reached its climax, a new and sinister plot began to unfold. Anika Bingham and Davillia Bonham, working in tandem with Victor Kandle, hatched a nefarious plan to permanently disable Sydney's quest and turn him to the dark side.

The sixteenth law, "The Law of Future Events," played a central role in this chapter. It posited that one's future events could be predicted with great accuracy and high probability based on past events. However, the further the event was into the future, the lesser the accuracy and probability of occurrence.

Anika and Davillia, harnessing their formidable powers, confronted Sydney with the intention of mesmerizing him and leading him down a path of darkness. Their hypnotic influence was overwhelming, and Sydney found himself ensnared in their web of manipulation.

As the chapter unfolded, Sydney's transformation into a dark and powerful entity named The Drago became apparent. He had turned to the dark side, drawn by promises of power and knowledge from Victor Kandle. The alliance between Victor and The Drago signalled a dangerous turning point in their quest.

Sydney's former allies, including Thunder Penguin, Haystacks, Ava Kristal, and Tara Krishana, tried desperately to bring him back to the side of light and truth. They invoked the sixteenth law, drawing upon the knowledge of past events and their deep connection with Sydney to steer him away from the abyss.

But their efforts were in vain. The Drago's newfound power was formidable, and his allegiance to Victor Kandle seemed unbreakable. The very laws of the universe seemed to bend to his will as he embraced the darkness that had once been a distant temptation.

The chapter reached its climax with a final, heart-wrenching confrontation between The Drago and his former allies. They pleaded with him to remember the journey they had undertaken together, the quest for truth that had brought them to this point.

Yet, as the chapter concluded, The Drago's resolve remained unyielding. He had turned to the dark side, and the fate of their quest hung in the balance. As the line between light and darkness blurred, and the ultimate showdown between The Drago, Victor Kandle, and The Shadow loomed on the horizon. The fate of the transcendent laws and the universe itself hung in the balance, and the story's final, major hook left no doubt that the climax of their journey was fast approaching.

Chapter 17

"Odes to Perfect Imperfections"

In the climactic final chapter of Sydney Korale's epic journey, the seventeenth law, "The Law of Perfect Imperfections," played a pivotal role. This profound law posited that the universe was manifested exactly as it should be, with perfect and mathematical precision. It suggested that the imperfections that existed were intentionally designed to complement the perfections around them. The very essence of the universe was a delicate balance between what humanity perceived as perfection and imperfection.

As the battle between The Shadow, Victor Kandle, and The Drago raged on, The Shadow invoked the seventeenth law to channel its power. It was a law that underscored the necessity of imperfections in the grand tapestry of existence, emphasizing that they were an integral part of the universe's design.

The Shadow's utilization of this law was a profound and symbolic gesture. It represented his belief in the imperfections of all beings, including Sydney himself, and his unwavering commitment to embracing those imperfections as part of the greater cosmic plan.

The battle that ensued was a testament to the interplay of perfections and imperfections. Each cosmic entity brought its unique strengths and weaknesses to the forefront, creating a dynamic struggle that resonated with the very essence of the seventeenth law.

As Sydney awoke from his hypnotic trance and returned to the bright side, he brought with him a renewed understanding of the seventeenth law. He realized that his imperfections were not weaknesses but rather facets of his humanity, and they, too, played a vital role in the balance of the universe.

With Sydney back on their side, The Shadow, and his allies, each embracing their own imperfections, faced Victor Kandle and his formidable cohorts. The battle was a grand spectacle, a symphony of cosmic forces embodying the perfection of their roles and the imperfections that made them unique.

Ultimately, it was the alliance of The Shadow, Sydney, and their allies that emerged victorious, not in spite of their imperfections but because of them. The forces of darkness and manipulation, represented by Victor and his allies, were defeated, and the transcendent laws were once again safeguarded.

With the battle concluded, the alliance turned their attention to the enigmatic figure of The Shadow. They sought to unearth the truth about his identity, to understand the cosmic being who had protected the balance of the universe throughout their journey.

But as they delved deeper into The Shadow's origins, they encountered a baffling enigma. The more they learned, the more questions arose. The identity of The Shadow remained shrouded in mystery, and his true nature remained elusive.

The quest for truth had led the alliance to the ultimate battle and victory, but the enigma of The Shadow's identity remained unresolved. The story concluded with the tantalizing promise that the mysteries of the transcendent laws and the universe itself were far from being fully understood.

Epilogue

"Dance of the Shadows"

The epilogue of Sydney Korale's extraordinary journey unfolded as an intricate tapestry, weaving together all seventeen key tenets of the transcendent laws in a mesmerizing revelation.

As the dust settled from the climactic battle between The Shadow, Sydney, and their allies against Victor Kandle and his malevolent cohorts, a profound moment of revelation awaited. The enigmatic figure known as The Shadow stepped forward, ready to unveil his true identity.

1. Energy is the Primeval Life Force: The Shadow, enveloped in an aura of pure energy, began to morph, its form shifting and shimmering.

2. The Law of Objects: Animate and inanimate objects alike seemed to resonate in harmony, attuned to the impending revelation.

3. The Law of Awareness: Awareness itself expanded, and Sydney, now fully awakened, could sense the depth of the moment.

4. The Thought Theorem: Thoughts danced in the air, forming a tapestry of ideas and intentions.

5. The Law of Communication: The very essence of communication enveloped the scene, connecting every being present.

6. The Brain-Heart Theory: The hearts of all resonated in unison, a symphony of emotions and understanding.

7. The Law of Scientific Prayer: The power of collective intent pulsed through the cosmos.

8. The Law of Data Availability: Information flowed freely, unlocking the secrets of the universe.

9. The Law of Synchronicity: The cosmic gears of destiny turned, aligning all beings and events.

10. The Law of Chaining: Threads of destiny intertwined, linking past, present, and future.

11. The Law of Action: Intent and execution merged into a singular force.

12. The Law of Lovelies: Love, unconditional and universal, flowed through every heart.

13. The Theorem of Divinity: The presence of divinity became palpable, transcending individual existence.

14. The Library of Universal Data: The collective wisdom of the universe shone brilliantly.

15. The Law of the Multiverse: The myriad possibilities of existence unfolded before their eyes.

16. The Law of Future Events: The future remained uncertain, a canvas yet to be painted.

17. The Law of Perfect Imperfections: Imperfections and perfections intertwined, creating a harmonious whole.

And then, in a final, stunning plot twist, The Shadow revealed his true identity. He was Sydney's father, long believed to have passed away. Sydney's shock and disbelief were palpable as he realized the depths of the cosmic journey he had undertaken. His father, an enlightened being, had been watching over him from the shadows, guiding him on a path toward truth and enlightenment.

The revelation of his father's identity shed light on the reasons behind The Shadow's actions. Sydney's father had long sought to protect his son and prepare him for the cosmic journey that lay ahead. He had harnessed the power of the transcendent laws to safeguard the universe and guide Sydney toward his destiny.

But the story did not end there. As Sydney and his father embraced, they turned their attention to Victor

Kandle, who lay half-dead, defeated and broken. Anika and Davillia had been banished into a realm of darkness.

Suddenly, out of nowhere, a figure emerged – The Queen Anastacia. With an air of sinister elegance, she revived Victor Kandle, her own dark agenda shrouded in mystery. The alliance watched in shock as Victor Kandle, now revived, stood alongside the enigmatic Queen Anastacia.

The shadow of uncertainty loomed over the destiny of the transcendent laws, the universe, and the fates of all the characters involved. The revelation of shadows had given way to new mysteries, and the promise of a second *act* beckoned with tantalizing possibilities.

Author Bio

Srinivas Krishnan is a dynamic author and thinker, renowned for his ability to intertwine complex scientific concepts with profound spiritual insights. With a background that merges academia and a deep-seated interest in metaphysical explorations, Krishnan's writing reflects a unique blend of knowledge and imagination. His works often delve into the mysteries of the universe, offering readers a thought-provoking journey through the realms of science and spirituality. Krishnan's storytelling is marked by its depth, engaging narrative style, and the ability to challenge and inspire his audience. He is celebrated for his ability to craft stories that are not only intellectually stimulating but also deeply resonant on a personal level, making him a distinguished figure in contemporary literature.

"IF YOU THINK
MONEY CAN'T
BUY HAPINESS
TRY BEING
BROKE"

~ SK ~

@KAIZENKRUNCHER

SRINIVAS KRISHNAN
EMPIRE K. INC

www.ingramcontent.com/pod-product-compliance
Lightning Source LLC
Chambersburg PA
CBHW030806180726
47991CB00024B/1098